To my own beloved family
Norm, Denny, Jules, Perry, Munro, Chuck,
Dorothy, Meg, Andrew, Kit, and Ian

—M.A.H.

Little, Brown and Company

Hachette Book Group USA
237 Park Avenue, New York, NY 10017
Visit our Web site at www.lb-kids.com

First Edition: August 2009

Library of Congress Cataloging-in-Publication Data

Hoberman, Mary Ann.
All kinds of families / by Mary Ann Hoberman ; illustrated by Marc
Boutavant. — 1st ed.
p. cm.
Summary: Rhyming text and illustrations explore the ways people,
animals, and even objects can form families.
ISBN 978-0-316-14633-3
[1. Stories in rhyme. 2. Family—Fiction.] I. Boutavant, Marc, ill.
II. Title.
PZ8.3.H66Aj 2009
[E]—dc22
2008016770

10 9 8 7 6 5 4 3 2 1

SCP

Printed in China

The illustrations for this book were done by digital media.
The text was set in AlineaIncise, and the display type was hand-lettered.

All Kinds of Families!

By Mary Ann Hoberman   Illustrated by Marc Boutavant

LITTLE, BROWN AND COMPANY
Books for Young Readers
New York   Boston

Families, families, all kinds of families
Families are people and animals, too
But all sorts of other things fit into families
Look all around and you'll see that they do!

A knife and a fork and a spoon are a family
The stars and the sun and the moon are a family
The socks in the drawer
And the rocks on the shore
And the blocks on the floor
They can all become families

Bottle caps, gingersnaps, buttons, or rings
You can make families from all sorts of things!

As soon as you're born, you're part of a family
As soon as you're born, you're a daughter or son
As soon as you're born, your family gets bigger
As soon as you're born, it is bigger by one

Eggs in a carton can seem like a family
So can a loaf with its slices of bread
Celery stalks or a big bunch of carrots
They sleep in the fridge with a drawer for a bed

What other things can you find to make families?
Thimbles and marbles and card decks and jacks
Ribbons and bobby pins, hair clips and thimbles
Pencils and rulers and crayons and tacks

Bottle caps, gingersnaps, buttons, or rings
You can make families from all sorts of things!

Clams in the sea make a clammily family
Lambs in the field make a lambily family
Jams in their jars make a jammily family
And yams in the cupboard a yammily family

Out in the yard you'll find dry twigs and branches
Horse chestnuts, barberries, acorns, and cones
Down at the beach you'll find pebbles and seashells
Soft-colored beach glass and ocean-smoothed stones

A saucer and cup can be brother and sister
A comb and a brush can be husband and wife
A plate and a bowl can be missus and mister
And so can the spoon or the fork or the knife

Your hand is a family, a family of fingers
Your foot is a family, a family of toes
And as you get older, each family gets older
And as you keep growing, each family grows

Bottle caps, gingersnaps, buttons, or rings
You can make families from all sorts of things!

If you are the first baby born to your mother
Your mother's a mother because you are here
If you are the first baby born to your father
Your father's a father because you appear

If you are the second one born in your family
Someone is a brother because you arrive
Or someone's a sister, and you are a sister
Or brother the moment that you are alive

You can make families from clay or from play dough
You can make families from mud or from snow
You can make families from paper or cardboard
Make them from sticks or balloons that you blow

Spools are a family
And tools are a family
And chalks for the blackboard at school are a family
Six slices of cheese or a pod full of peas
Or a key ring with keys
They can all become families

Bottle caps, gingersnaps, buttons, or rings
You can make families from all sorts of things!

As soon as you're born, you might make a new grandma
Or maybe a grandpa, that's what you might do
You might make a cousin; you might be a cousin
An uncle or aunt might be made just by you

Pens full of bright-colored ink are a family
Toothbrushes over the sink are a family
Even the thoughts that you think are a family
Light as a feather
Living together
Inside of your mind
What else can you find?

You might say that numbers belong in a family
Or alphabet letters or notes in the scale
The colors in rainbows, the words in a language
The keys on a piano or stamps for the mail

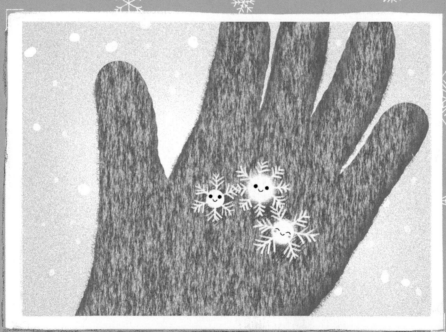

Inside or outside in summer or winter
You can find families for so many games
Families to play with, spend most of the day with
Telling them stories and giving them names

Bottle caps, gingersnaps, buttons, or rings
You can make families from all sorts of things!

Make-believe families and families of people
Families of people from long, long ago
Families like stepping stones crossing the water
Leading to now and the families you know

Everyone comes from a number of families
When you look backward, it looks like a tree
People from families make other new families
The more you go back, the more people you see

Play families, real families, all kinds of families
Think of the families, the ones that you're from
Someday you'll grow up and you'll have a new family
And you'll be the family of families to come!